The young boy pushed through the two heavy glass doors that lead to the waiting area of the upscale evening lounge. Before making it all the way inside he turned to make sure he made a couple finger smudges on the glass doors. He then sat his black worn duffle bag of hustle materials next to him on the floor as he took in the setting of the waiting room. It was dark and quiet but he knew somebody had to be there. Cars were outside in the back and two high end whips sat in the front. The young boy looked through the curtains that lead into the interior of the club. "Hello? Hello where everybody at? It's money at door." the young boy sang sung as loud as he could then laughing at himself. A voice came from the right of him that made him jump but he didn't pull his head back. He turned to see a well-dressed young black boy that couldn't have been that much older than him.

"What's up jitt you lost?"

"I'm looking for the manager"

"Well you seem a little too young to be making reservations or asking for a job, so what you want with the manager?"

"I like to keep that between the manager and I if that is alright with you?"

"Look I handle a lot of his business so I'll pass it on whatever it is and I'll also make it priority."

"Okay what is the manager name?"

"Mr. Green, Daniel Green."

"Okay well I have a proposition for Mr. Green I'll come do all his glass, and he got a lot in here. Every Monday on the dot for one hundred fifty dollars. I noticed these front doors were a little icky when I came in so I'll clean this now to give you an idea of how well I do my job. Oh and I'll come in the same time he comes in or earlier and get the job done quickly." The boy went through his bag pulling out a spray bottle towels and a squeegee. He cleaned the door he intentionally smudged and wiped down the other door just for kicks. He turned back toward the man. "So what do you think? So clean somebody might break they face tryna walk through."

"We don't need that lawsuit."

"You aint lying the way the world work somebody can sue they momma for giving birth to em." The man laughed at the boys' candidness. "So you are going talk to the boss right?"

"You got a job. I could never be mad or stop a young brother with a hustle. Come in Sunday Morning ten a.m. and my doors wouldn't have been dirty if you kept your little paw prints off of them."

"Yo doors?"

"I'm Daniel Green you can call me Daniel. What is your name?"

"I'm Mann or Mann Man whatever. You own this? You look so young you look about my age if not two or three years older max?"

"Age aint nothing but a number it's the dedication that matter. Be here ten a.m. sharp."

The teen boy face shot up with glee "Thank you for the opportunity Daniel." he pulled the heavy glass open making sure not to touch any part of it with his bag on his shoulder as he jetted off proud of himself. Next he would try and secure a job within the business. Daniel watched as the boy ran off looking like he held a million dollar ticket. Little did he know he actually did secure that ticket as soon as he walked in the Lounge and presented himself.

He wondered what the young boy had been through or escaped to be where he was right now. So many kids ran to the streets for shelter only to find the streets didn't shelter anybody or anything. But if you were lucky you may find somebody with a good heart that would put you over and beyond.

Derek who everybody called BD except for his ladies that called him Big Daddy. He was the kind man with the good heart that Daniel had to thank. BD took Daniel under his wing when he was a jitt. He had been in and out of foster care twice. He didn't like the families CPS put him under so both of them he removed himself away from. The first time he ran away he got located days later where they held him till they found him somewhere else to go. The next and last time he left he made sure they would never find him again. He just couldn't get down with their lifestyle or having the extra kids around with the lame excuse of family activity, he wasn't rocking with it. After about three months of being on the streets after leaving the second family and running back to the hood he was raised in and used to he felt better, not happy but better.

BD walked up on him right while he was picking through Barbeque City dumpster. It was a clear night smelled like it was going to rain though so he was moving fast so he could seek shelter when he heard his name called. "Daniel!" He bout shitted his pants at the sound of his name being called he just stood there maybe they would go away. "Aye lil nigga don't freeze now. I aint the police." Daniel turned to see who it was. "Get yo ass up out the trash bin boy." Daniel turned back around to continue his search he didn't have time to be playin with people. "Aye let me get you some real food."

"This is real food, dogs and cats aint supposed to eat this shit nigga." Daniel spat in a low tone cutting his eyes. BD held up his hands as to surrender with a smirk on his face.

"It's true I don't want any trouble lil potna. How about you let me get you some hot food then? That's all I really meant. I got an order I'm picking up from here anyway that they holding for me. I'll have them add you a plate too."

Daniel pulled himself up erect dropping the bag in hand. He turned to look BD right in the eyes before beginning to walk towards him. A satisfied BD turned and began walking towards the front door where security unlocked the door.

"BD what's good with cha my man?"

"Shid bout to get some of this good food after a good day of work"

"It's true taking mine home with me because if I bus down here I aint gone be securing shit but a tap out."

"That's real I feel you." BD looked back checking for Daniel before walking through the door. That's when security noticed Daniel then took his attention back to BD. "I need a plate for my little potna too."

"You and Mary gone have to work that one out but I'm sure you got that under control."

"I'm sure I do." They dabbed each other and smiled then security locked the door behind him. "Go wash yo hands jitt I know where they been." BD giggled as Daniel made his way the bathroom. "These young niggas out of control S.G."

"Tell me about it I deal with they mild mannered asses everyday no type of home training."

While in the bathroom Daniel washed his hands then decided to do a quick sink wash down. He went to clean his shoes the best he could then stashed some paper towels in his pockets for whenever he may have needed them. When he walked back out there was two to go plates and cups stacked and sitting on the table and the lady Mary was talking to BD. Daniel knew who she was because her and his momma always talked for long ass lengths when they went there for food. When she saw Daniel she smiled did a slight wave then kissed BD on the cheek then disappearing back into the kitchen.

"Welcome back lil nigga what you was doing taking a shower. Look first thigs first always keep ya hands clean and nails clipped. Let me see yo hands." Daniel showed him his hands flipping them over both ways.

"I know."

"Second. Go get me a coke light ice and whatever it is that you drink." Daniel did what he was told getting himself the grape Kool aide they had. He took the drinks to the table then went back to get napkins and straws.

"You want a toothpick?" Daniel asked placing a few in his pocket along with some wet wipes.

"Yea" BD checked his drink to make sure Daniel listen then began with the interrogation. "I know for a fact you don't belong over here anymore homie"

"I belong wherever my feet take me."

"Did your feet run away from your new momma and daddy?"

"Aint no such a thing"

"What you mean aint no such thing? What, of running or having a new mommy and daddy." Daniel stopped eating and looked at BD who was glaring with a smirk wiping his fingers with his elbows rested on the table.

"Both." Daniel answered focusing back on his hot familiar meal. Three months ago he couldn't have eaten this whole meal, half way through he would have been full packing it up to take home. Tonight though it was a different story he was far from full. He felt like it wouldn't even hold him over before he was digging in somebodies trash again.

"You miss your moms and pops huh? Daniel just gave him a look. "So you just gone do it on your own?" Daniel shrugged his shoulder as if to say yea. "Oh so you don't need anybody, no cloths, no money, no bed, no nothing, huh?"

"Not at the moment."

BD belched a laugh that came from deep within causing his head to push back and body shake back and forth. He wiped his mouth then dropped his napkin down to reach for his phone in his back pocket. He was still chuckling while dialing a number glancing at Daniel who was about finished with his plate. He listened while he waited "Yo baby get the guest room together for me we got a guest coming to stay a while." He hung up the phone throwing money on the table "Mary we gone have to link up another time baby." BD yelled towards the kitchen.

"You aint shit nigga you know that?"

"You mean Iam the shit?"

"You better be happy you got that baby with you."

"No you better be happy I got this baby with me." He turned his attention back to Daniel. "What size shoes you wear?"

"Size eight."

"I'm coming for my plate tomorrow night."

"We closed." Mary yelled back out causing BD to laugh and shake his head.

"Alright let's go. I gotta make a stop over to somebodies house real quick then we can get some shut eye. Remember to always handle whatever it is on your mind if it is obtainable take care of it then and there don't wait till later. You want to live easy not hard. Handle your business don't stack it. Understood?

"Yea"

BD hoped out the car jetting inside he was maybe in there for ten minutes the most before caming back out. He held two big plastic shopping bags one filled with plain tee shirts black and white the other bag filled with jeans and black sweat pants. In his other hand he held two Nike shoe boxes black and white. "You never want to stand out but blend in. It's not what you wear it's how you wear it. It's about the cleanliness of it don't be sloppy don't be dirty. Keep it clean tight and stand up straight. That's the key." Daniel shook his head as to say got it. BD just drove in silence no music no talking he just rode. That moment reminded him of time with his mother it was his dad that always had to have some type of noise or sound going on.

Daniel leaned back in his seat finally relaxing his body and just took in the scenery it was the same but now slightly different maybe because he had really been in it. He wasn't just an observer anymore now he was a walking entity of it. He had really been in them seen and experienced somethings he and his parents would just watch on television together. He knew BD and his reputation he didn't know him personally but he knew everybody knew him, even his mom and dad knew him. He had seen in the past how he looked at his mom on a few occasions watching their interactions and conversations. Daniel wasn't on that right now he wanted to just chill and relax not worry about what he was ultimately getting his self into because he knew he was stepping into something and tomorrow he would handle it. Right now he was experiencing what his dad described as the itis after every meal. His eyes flicked open and close to the smooth comfortable silent ride it had been a while since he just floated.

"Concrete" BD spoke startling him from his relaxed state. "Concrete that's your new name. Anybody ask that's what you tell em every time you introduce yourself which really I wouldn't just walk around introducing myself because government or not I don't like people tagging me. Shit you might find a lil lady you want to talk to I don't know either way your name is Concrete. Even when she say no what's your government tell her fast ass to chill or least get to know her first. You don't have a last name if they looking for a last name they probably looking for trouble. Your new family and I will be calling you Concrete for now on. Someday down the road you may have another tag but I'll tell you that one when the time comes. Do you understand?" That was all the Daniel needed to hear to confirm what he already knew he was now Concrete BD property.

"Yes Sir."

CONCRETE

Chapter two

"I never stole a dime from you. I mean why would I? I have no reason to I've been loyal to you from the day you brought me into this family."

"Look all I know is I can't be in Miami that's why I got you to take care of that entire situation while I'm up here handling this entire situation."

"Look Julio said everything checked out. He's been working for us along time I figured he know what he was talking about."

"A whole fifty grand how does a whole fifty grand get by someone? Even if you didn't count that's a weight change. You should have noticed that as many times you picked up that bag. How many times you done picked up this bag, how many times this bag been sitting next to you? So you could have recounted or just paid attention to the weight you did nothing." Concrete sat back in his chair he liked Pedro, he had been working with him for years. He wanted to give him the benefit of doubt. "Pedro I know you getting a little older not as sharp as you use to be right?"

"I aint getting that damn old. I messed up so wh…"

"I'm sorry" Concrete lifted the gun from his lap shooting Pedro in the head. "Nigga wanna debate like he got life-lines and shit I don't have time for that mess. Call Miami and tell Juan it's his now. He owes me a fifty five thousand advance. Please get his old ass out my office and order me another one of those rugs after you call my cleaning team."

"On it boss."

Concrete hated doing street business in his legit spots but sometimes it called for it sometimes you just had to throw the trash out wherever you were at it just couldn't wait because it smelled that bad. He looked at Pedro lifeless body and shook his head. Why can't folk just handle they business why so greedy? What you get out it nothing at all? Running my shit like it's his and since he can't act like he got common sense his family won't even have a decent funeral cause all they gone get is his head. Concrete hated to do it but since he was hour's away people had to be made and sent as messages. He walked to his lounge seat leaning back into it raising his feet and pulling out a tin can that sat in the breast of his suit jacket which he removed and place over a chair right next to his desk. He removed a tightly rolled dobbie from the tin that smelled of gorilla glue. He lit the tip and inhaled.

"Yo boss sorry to bother you but it's a jitt outside talking bout he work for you and I'm messing up his check." Concrete sat up putting out his blunt and reached to retrieve is his jacket.

"Oh yea let little man in, I forgot all about jitt coming through today. I be out there in a minute"

"Lil nigga got a smart ass mouth."

"Yea he is a smart ass. When yall take the body over there just feed em everything but the head and make sure you get his wedding ring."

"Yes..."

"And don't come back by here today my workers get nervous around yall big niggas"

"Let that Sandra know I'm just here to protect her"

"I done told you Daniel's and Concrete's employees are two different worlds they cannot mingle."

"I know I know" Concrete left his experts to clean up his mess while he got back into Daniel mode.

"Hey young man you on time. I love that."

"Man ya goons tried to mess that up for me. Since he was playing with me I did a quick lil roast session on his ass must of cut him close I see he aint come back for more" Concrete laughed from deep within.

"Mann you feisty remind me of somebody I once knew."

"That somebody people be talking about whenever they say *you remind me of somebody* they be talking about themselves or someone they love. So who am I reminding you of? You or somebody you love?" Concrete smiled at the young man he liked him and was happy he stopped to see him days ago.

"I know you here to do windows but let's take a ride."

"Do I still get paid?"

"Yea."

"Then let's ride. Can I take my bike in the lounge so it don't get stolen?"

"Yea, yo before we open somebody make sure to take his bike and lock it up in the back room with his work supplies. Alright little potna lets ride."

What Mann didn't know is that Concrete did his research on him too. Concrete knew what Mann was capable of, he knew who he was first day they officially met in the lounge. He had heard of him the streets was talking about him, even seen him freestyle on two different videos on Instagram. He knew his government was Emanuel Grant he was fifteen never knew his mom and his dad was an active drug attic. He was the only child became a high school dropout last year and recently got his present girlfriend pregnant. Mann stood about 5'9 chocolate knotty hair that hadn't had a brush or comb thru it in what looked like forever. His clothes fit kind of big you could tell they were hand me downs. No odor came from him so he knew he had a stable roof over his head.

"Oh shit is this Concrete Lotus Ent?" Mann exclaimed as the gated fence opened up for them to pull in

"The one and only. Come on."

"Oh man I would forget my phone at home the day I go to Concrete Lotus ain't nobody gone believe this shit here."

"You can take pictures next time you up here." Concrete used his key card to open the door.

"Oh shit you connected like that? You got a key and shit and what you mean next time? I'm up here am I cleaning this place too?" Mann eyes were scanning the whole building he was cheesing big ass shit "Okay naw it's cool, as long as you pay I don't got a problem." A man greeted Concrete

"Sup boss." The two dabbed each other Concrete motioned towards Mann while still doing something in his phone.

"This him right here take him back there and see what he can do. Aye yo Mann go ahead and follow him I'll be around."

"What the fuck is going on round here?" Mann stated following the man enthusiastically bouncing up and down "You Golddrum the producer I follow you on Instagram. What the fuck is this some type of sick joke?"

Concrete knew he would like that he seen the hustle and heart in his words on the IG video and the hustle about the windows confirmed what he already knew. Concrete had always wanted to do something with music since he could remember he loved the way music would shimmer on your skin kissing you ever so lightly. How a soulful singer could pull all your emotions pain or happiness to the core. How a family reunion song made you want to laugh and dance all night with your family bringing you a state euphoria. Or how a freaky song would make you want to get up and shake your booty.

He loved that feeling. He remembered the effect music had on his parents. One minute his parents could be mad but a song a tune could make them forget all the anger they just threw at each other and just want to hug laugh and talk again. When he watched a performer he loved to see the joy on their face. The humbleness the surprise or disbelief that those people in the audience are here watching them do something they absolutely love and think of as fun. When he seen Mann he had only seen two videos but in those two one minute videos he seen a man in love with art. The way he crafted his words and delivery made me hungry for more, each video he had to watch about ten times in one sitting. So when that young man came to his lounge his hunger and determination popped up again and Concrete figured it was time for him to pay it forward.

Concrete lost his parents to the drug game or at least that's what he believed it to be at the age of eight. One of those nights when after a long day of work when parents just put the kids up turn on music and enjoy your significant other night. Nights some or many parents don't get enough of. The two of them rocking and swaying in each other arms with a quick disconnect to take a sip or a pull of a doobie. Most nights Concrete would take a while to fall asleep because he would lie in bed and be singing and humming the songs too. He really did love music. On that particular night it was a breeze to fall asleep in fact it rushed him. It was a knock at the door that grew louder and louder woke Concrete out of his sleep. He knew whoever it was had to just be getting the attention of his parents since the sounds of the Isley Brothers were blaring through the house. The music went down a few octaves then the talking began everything was mixed up like an ongoing mumble Concrete really couldn't tell what was being said. He began to drift off again. The light conversation abruptly turned into loud yelling which now had Concrete in the upright position trying hard to hear past the music and at least make out the extra voices downstairs. When this didn't work to his approval he crept to the top of the stairs which seemed to have taken forever being he didn't want to make the slightest sound. He even crawl thinking that would make it even easier to creep. He didn't know if he was scared to get in trouble by his parents if he got caught out of bed or what but something in his gut said do not make a sound. When he made to the end of the wall he took a deep breath peeking around the corner and down the stairs. He froze when he saw three guns pointing at his parents he felt like he was going to pass out he wondered did the gunman know that they had a kid or if he was even there nobody looked for him yet maybe they would let his parents live. Concrete made his way to his parent's room in a daze crawling still; He grabbed the phone off their night stand the crawled on the side of the bed that shield him from view. He dialed a number.

"Hello 9-1-1 what's the emergency?"

"They're going to kill my mommy and daddy."

"Who is? Where are you at now?"

"Three men, I'm at home in Robles Park."

"What is your name?"

"Daniel I have to go now."

He crept back the stair case listening and watching everything. He watched to Stephanie Mills Home playing in the back ground.

"Daniel you own Concrete Lotus Ent.?" Mann asked smiling coming from the back with the producer.

"Part owner."

"Wow I can't believe this I went to Key lounge hopping to work my way into the restaurant business and that move got me doing something I would kill to have a shot at. You heard me I would kill not to do but just to have a shot. You understand the difference?"

"You may be shocked but I do my brother. That's why you are here right now."

"So what you want from me in order to live my dream? I know you want something everybody want something."

"Right now just think of me ass your fairy godfather I just want to look out and help. I love music so how can I not love a true creator of it."

"Bet."

"Only thing I need is for you to start going back to school I will house you and your girlfriend. Yall will have curfews. She has to continue working until and then go right back after. Yall still have responsibilities and a life to live. I'm not here to support you I'm just going to make it slightly easier."

"Okay, bet." Mann smiled shaking hands.

"This is like a deal with the devil don't cross me. I'm here for your future I'm giving money space and time.

You take it for granted then you may be taken for granted.
You understand?"

"This all I ever wanted to do, I'm a good
investment."

"I usually know how to pick em."

Chapter three

Over the years Concrete had changed he was definitely what most would call a snack. He was the perfect shade a brown like the brown crayon out the box. He was tall reaching a mere 6'3 feet tall he wore deep setting dimples in both cheeks that you could get a peek at even if he wasn't smiling. He had two gold teeth up top and four at the bottom not pull outs it was a family tradition to get them done after high school graduation. He had full lips a little on the dark side from smoking some much weed smooth skin and locs some colored by the sun others switched by bleach that reached his waist. The night his parents left changed his life and the path it would take. Even though he did wrong he tried to balance it out with the good. From the lounge a place for the black or urban community to vibe. The studio a place for people to express themselves make money and potentially even be pulled up out the hood. Even the cars he flipped he bought good low mileage vehicles and sale them dirt cheap to single parents grandparents college students people that actually needed and could really use good transportation. The jobs at his business were real employees not his street workers he tried to keep the two as separate as the name Daniel and Concrete.

He let his business partner be the face of Concrete Lotus Ent she was an artist sexy and she loved music if not as much more than he so that was perfect. As far as the lounge he looked so young no one would believe he owned it so he acted as a general manager. The car shop was just a store front a place to keep the cars he flipped a place to flip money. When it came down to the game he didn't have to worry about nothing everything was sealed tight all the years running he never had a problem his name did numbers and that was all that it was to that.

Concrete sat in his Condo that looked over Downtown Tampa in a high-rise. He liked to look down and watch the people go on and about their daily hustle. No matter what day what time whatever he could always find somebody moving like clockwork. Watching everybody from the white and blue collar workers to the panhandlers down to your average house mom or dad. Almost everybody that was downtown had a routine some may have fooled him but he pretty much had them down. It is crazy how people can do the same thing every day down to the same time always keeps the same moves not even realizing they could be being read like a book setting up their own failure.

Concrete didn't want that he didn't want to be known or read like someone's favorite book. He like blending in never standing out he like what some called him as unpredictable. He inhaled his blunt blowing what didn't fit in his lungs out the crack of the window. He practiced on making circles Niecy could role her tongue just right and make all different sizes of circles. He spotted X pulling in the parking garage. X was Concretes right hand man he had linked up with X maybe after two or three years of working for BD one day BD just put em together and was like yall bothers now so act like it. Neither of them were stupid so what BD said it was had to be for something and it was. Together their minds worked like well-oiled machinery quiet and efficient. Whatever one wasn't with the other was and when it was a hell no from the gut it was a hell no for the both of them. They didn't lie they didn't steal they just got money. X was just in the dope game he didn't want in on the legit paying taxes life he just wanted to stay under the radar and live like the white folk worry free. That's why he called him over because he had plans and X was a big part of them.

"Honey I'm home." X sang through the house shutting the door right behind him then heading to the fridge next. Niecy always kept the fridge stocked with water and a variety of fruit he grabbed bottled water. "Aye Concrete where you at nigga."

"Damn can a man shit in peace what you do run up here?"

"Damn near."

"Look business first then all that other shit."

"Handle it."

"Niecy is pregnant."

"Congratulations bro."

"Thank you, thank you man we happy." Concrete took a deep breath "I'm getting out the game for good. I done set up everything where you will meet the plug and everybody else that you didn't know was a part of the team. No more than two weeks I will be gone and everything will be handled by you. I just want out I don't want my child to lose me or my wife for some stupid shit. I still don't even know why my folks were killed I can't let my child or children feel the same void. We live pretty vicious lives at times I do well just me and Niecy but bringing a child in the mix can really complicate and slow things down. I'll be around cause of the club and studio you know I need my income too but once you are in I will be out."

"Damn nigga whatever you want to do but damn could nigga at least get a month."

"You know you just got to do it handle it in this game can't do too much thinking. Plus shit was looking kind of crazy in some areas. I had to fix that but everything is good now we should have a smooth transition with a good team no problems."

"It's true." X mind was going a mile minute he had so many questions but the door opened and in came Niecy he knew when Niecy was around Concrete talked no business whatsoever. She aint know where the trap houses were she didn't know about the car shop she knew of nobody outside of X, BD and Stunna. She didn't pick up money stash drugs drive him anywhere never even heard him say the word drugs. Concrete wanted her dead to everything that was going on the less she knew the better he felt. Anywhere she would be no drugs were allowed minus the weed they both inhaled. As far as he was concerned his lady wasn't aware of his drug activity. She knew he went by Concrete but she always called him Daniel and his three friends were just that friends. X knew the back story of Niecy and what she meant to him he understood why his bro-friend kept her so safe and unaware while staying a loyal one woman man. He appreciated their relationship.

"Uh oh what I walk into yall both quiet and looking stupid."

"He always is acting like that whenever you come around. I don't know if he in love or scared of ya ass."

"It better be both." She said grabbing Concrete face to plant a kiss on his lips.

"Anyways what up Niecy how you doing sis?" X said."

"Shit you know same shit different day. Happy Birthday young man!!"

"Awe thank you Niecy." X was genuinely happy she was the first one to say Happy Birthday to him today. "My guy here didn't even tell me that."

"Man I was getting to that."

"Dis nigga."

"X what are you doing over here so early on your special day? What you up here doing tryna get my man out tonight and round some hoochies?" She laughed rubbing her barley there stomach.

"Even if I did make that happen it wouldn't last long. He wouldn't be worried about a damn thang but some money."

"That's a lie them hoes would make him sick bringing him home to his real fix."

"No lies told at all." Concrete said smiling at Niecy.

"I know. Anyways I'm about to go hop in the shower. That sun aint no joke and that humidity aint no hoe...at ease boys."

"Shit I'm about to hop in the shower too."

"Yall nasty and all in love head asses. Ima holla at you two freak hoes later. Oh yea congratulations on the pregnancy Niecy." Niecy looked at Concrete tapping him in the shoulder with her fist making a face like why you told then rolled her eyes.

"Thank you boo you be good today."

"Everyday sis."

Back down stairs X hoped in his whip on cloud nine he knew he was about to be getting paid now. He had been getting paid but he didn't do as much a Concrete he didn't meet the plug with Concrete they was a unit but not a team.

27

X didn't never really care about that because he ate and it was hefty plus Concrete was always fair. He never felt like he worked for him and Concrete never bragged he was really like a brother.

X didn't know all the details but he knew if Concrete said it then shit was real. He knew now he had to make some silent moves and get brand new everything not new not fancy just different then what everybody use to it was time to hide in plain sight. Get brand new with the change because it would be on a whole other level.

X pulled up to his first trap house check of the day. He parked watching the movement for a minute or two then stepped out making a whistle that was this month's signal for whoever needed to go inside with him to follow lead. Once inside he sat down and waited looking around at the sheets and blankets on the walls the ashtrays and homemade ashtrays that spilled over with ashes roaches cigarettes and black and mild's. Mix matched interior it was just chaotic how young boys were with no motherly supervision it was dark the smell was stale and everything looked dirty no matter how good the jay they paid with dope did cleaning up the spot. No doubt about it being in any trap houses gave him anxiety. He always wondered how the girls he use to get to come chill with him even put up with the shit you got different niggas pulling in and out. All kind of fiends knocking and the dogs barking that stayed on alert.

He hated being in them that's all you had to do to be linked to anything. Just show face and be present and bam some type of surveillance or possible pending case. He was happy to be taking Concretes place and giving someone else the responsibility of doing this important but petty stuff and dangerous stuff.

"Yo X what's good with you bro?" the little homie Squirt came in looking all red and winded.

"Aint nothing just picking up chickens."

"Bout that…we got hit last night."

"What?"

"Somebody ran through here last night."

"Who was here when it happened?"

"Nobody" X was standing now he was no longer sitting on the edge of the couch.

"Nobody? Was all the work gone?"

"No."

"Then why the fuck nobody was here working last night? It should always be somebody here when it is money in here to be made."

"It was a par…"

"Don't even finish that sentence, you sound like you bout to say some dumb shit. What about the other trap houses any of them get hit?"

"No"

"Why the fuck nobody called me when yall found out all our shit gone? How much money and how much dope?"

"Yo collection for the day and half a kilo coke some molly and pound a weed."

"What the fuck, who all work this spot again?"

"Fatz Rell Con and me."

"If you niggas aint gone be here don't yall know to at least hide the shit. Yall supposed to find a dope ass hiding spot in plain sight. What yall just leaving shit on the table and shit in plain sight like this not the hood. Who does that shit jitt?"

"We aint never had to think about no shit like this. Nobody doesn't ever mess with us."

"Well good thing yall wasn't here, would yall even have been ready for war? Look you get ya squad together meet me at Tillies today at four pm."

"Bet. But what about work what we pose to tell clientele."

"I don't know tell em the truth yall fucked up."

X couldn't believe this shit just happened like that these young niggas done either got greedy or they really some cum dumb happy bastards. Concrete was going to be pissed about this, twenty five bands was a big lose. In all the time they had been in the game together they never experienced getting robbed or fucked by anyone. They were the ones to flip shit to where nobody even thought to do such things. It was twelve fourteen now it was time for X to do some quick investigations on all the little niggas that ran that spot see if anybody was acting strange or above they pay range. First he had to run by their other houses because in this game you never knew.

X got in the game when he was twelve he came from a good family both parents still very much alive they were just too strict on him and he didn't particularly like that. X had always been a big boy weight wise but when he was younger it was that bad weight that *you so big that* or *you so fat that* or *you're lil sloppy joe*. Man kids were the worst who loved to taunt you and the ones with the weight were their favorite. Just because he moved a little slow and breathed a little funny. He was all those things but he also fast he could run slap punch kick a bitch before they seen it coming. The hate from the kids and all the rules and regulations from his parents made X say fuck everybody all yall ass could kick rocks. At the age of eleven he ran away. He started off doing shoplifting mostly for food and small expensive things he could sell on the street moving to pick pocketing. When he felt his face was becoming known especially for never purchasing anything. He would even pickpocket the elderly busy men and women. He acted as if he were helping at that moment but he was working. For anyone who just got to damn close and invaded his space they became a victim too.

One night he was at this big block party it was crowed everybody who was anybody was there it lasted from at least two pm to the wee hours of the night. X was tired but he knew it was money all around he had made about twenty seven hundred already off these drunken happy go lucky fools. Nobody paid attention to children especially fat ones so when he bumped or touched them he assumed they just blamed his fatness or him just being a careless kid.

X was sitting on the curb paying close attention to this one cat that was known in the streets big time he had a well-known rep. When the opportunity presented itself X would go in to make himself known. Some song was on that had everybody riled up and the chicks were showing out so it was X time. He did what in his head was a dance and hoped it appeared to be one to anyone else who may have stolen a glance of him. X slide in the open car door pulling his keys and phone then brushed past him lifting his wallet. X sashayed back to the curb he had been chillin on just watching the dude until finally "Aye who got my shit!" The man he pocketed said not yelling but speaking loud enough for people around him to hear. "What shit" another man replied "Did I give my shit to somebody? I don't remember giving my shit up." Dude placed his drink on the car and blunt in mouth beginning to pat himself down with a confused look on his face. He then opened the car door wider and just sat there still looking stupid. "Did I bring it out the house…of course I did how else I drove my car." The man stepped out the car looking around at everybody a few watched him the rest continued about their business. "Okay which one of yall mother fuckers playing with me? Hmm cause I aint that drunk." He said lifting his cup shaking it a little. "Matter fact…" That's when X finally stepped in. "Big dawg?"

"What's up jitt you seen somebody sneaking round me yo ass been sitting there all night" X looked around and met a couple eyes that were asking the same question but with a little more intensity then man himself had actually asked.

"Naw" X shook his head watching the heads turn from him "Well what yo big head ass want?" X smiled maybe because it felt good not to be called fat ass or big boned. When the man called him big head it reminded him of his uncle. X walked over to the man keeping space while talking low but loud enough for the man to hear.

"Listen here Unk can I get a place on your team I'm homeless I'm out just trying to survive I'm smart I may not look like it but I'm fast too." The man whole body was facing X now.

"What you asking me lil man? What you want be me or be like me, what can you do for me? You coming up to me asking for a job and I don't even know or ever seen you before a day in my life. You haven't helped me so I don't owe you anything at all. You been sitting in that same spot over there for about four hours just watching and you aint seen nothing happen round me? Sounds to me I don't need you like my grandma use to say. I can do bad all by my damn self, fuck em."

"See I knew you say that I expected it actually so I aint even booty hurt by what you just said. I told you I'm smart and fast." X reached in his pockets pulling out his keys wallet and phone.

"What about now?" The man pulled his cup from his mouth sitting it back on top of his car pulling his blunt from behind his ears before he lit it.

"What's yo name big head?"

"Xavier" The man sat and looked at him for a minute while inhaling and exhaling.

"Alright then X. Nice to meet yo lil homie I'm BD." Ever since he been in this game or this family he liked to call it. Any and everything his name was attached to was straight so for some shit to go down as far as a robbery at only one location made him feel like somebody was trying his gangsta. The only thing to do now was find out who it was. He never went to Concrete with half a story.

Chapter four

Concrete drove on the interstate in silence he liked silence. He hated driving but most importantly he hated leaving his lady behind so much. He hated watching his back every damn day and night. He hated worrying about who was eating or who was in they feeling. When he got in these moods the best thing for him was his lady or a ride in the silence. Unfortunately for him he had just left his lady and this ride wasn't just a night or day drive this was a *I gotta go handle business and make boss moves* drive. A part of the life that he disliked even more and that gave him even excessive stress.

Concrete pulled up Tillies and sat a few seconds later the garage door started up and Concrete drove forward on the inside. He seen X car parked straight ahead to the left and he didn't see X but Stunna was leaning on the back of his truck playing with his phone in one hand and his gun in the other. Concrete parked making his way to Stunna giving him dap

"Stunt what's up man where X at?"

"Somewhere round here complaining about birthday sex or some shit nigga look like he wanna cry and shit talking about stupid ass kids and all this other bullshit. I told him since he knows what's up we can handle this quick and you don't even have to come down. He wasn't wit it so here we are."

"I'm right here Concrete nigga knew I was in the car he just wanted to talk shit you know how that nigga get. It's got to be that short nigga complex and shit." Concrete walked over to X dabbing him up.

"Having a hell of a birthday huh? So what happened earlier?"

"Went to go get the pickups first house I hit over there in Nuccio. Squirt tells me he doesn't have the money cause they was hit last night."

"Last night?"

"Same shit I said then the nigga opens his mouth to say nobody was there. They all had stepped out and then on top of that the nigga say no other houses got touched or nothing."

"So somebody stealing from they own family."

"See we on the same page. So I go to check up on these niggas Squirt in the clear he was about to shit himself telling me this shit that youngin good. So I get to Cons house him and Rell outside in the front squaring up."

"For what"

"Aye you aint tell me this shit them lil boney ass niggas was prolly both missing connecting with air." Stunna chimed in

"So I roll my window down to see what they saying cause they throwing words with them hands, and them little motha fuckers was connecting they got hands. Well it kind look like they was slap boxing. Anyways Rell talking about fuck you that was a team effort what you did was wrong. Con talking about fuck the team I am the team and all this shit. I got tired of watchin them niggas so I pulled up on Fatz. He was sitting outside eating asked why he wasn't working he said I'm working on staying fat, I gets mine. Told him he and the three idiots need to meet at Tillies at 4pm. He nodded I speed off."

"The question is am I going to have to kill somebody tonight?"

"The answer is yes."

"I wish these little niggas would hurry up it aint like they out making no money. Watch what I say we gone see them pull up in exactly thirty minutes." Stunna said shaking his head in disgust "These young niggas got no ambition at all. I know there're somewhere thinking they coming up with the perfect lie. I bet you."

Concrete walked up the stairs of the warehouse into what used to be BD office but was now his. All the equipment was gutted and dated and it looked like they ran a legit audio service when in reality this was just the garage he used to store the cars he flipped another source of good income and way to run shit without being noticed driving the same whip. The shop was also where things that were considered bad or expired were taken. Those things that needed to disappear was brought here to be disposed of. Only a few knew of the disposal part and the ones that did know dared not to tell.

Sometimes you gotta do with your left hand what you would normally do with your right. Your right hand is the one you can count on but your left hand is the one no one is watching. This played in Concrete head whenever he was about to kill because that's what BD told him on his sweet sixteen the day he became a man. A man of the streets.

He and BD sat in the upstairs office while BD handled papers and move some things around Concrete watched the cameras that filmed outside the garage.

"Concrete you always asking me to bring you to the shop. You see aint nothing special about this place its dirty big dark and smell like the no good cigarette smoking uncle everybody got."

"Well where is everybody at, the workers?"

"They ass better be somewhere working. You will understand one day when all this is yours." Concrete looked at BD eyes wide. "What you looking like that for you done showed and prove in the last couple of years you been working with me you took over blocks and out ranked workers above you. You got heart I don't know if it's because of what you seen or what you always had in you. With your sweet sixteen hitting in less than thirty minutes it's time for you to show and prove but never tell and I'm gone make it real easy for you."

"My daddy told me when you fend for yourself pay yo own way and move without asking then you a man so in my eyes and my daddy's I think I been a man."

"I damn sure can't argue with you on that you been carrying yourself like G since the day I pulled you out the trash can." Concrete laughed.

"Man you aint pull me out of shit. You were begging to take me to dinner so I accepted." They both laughed then Concrete started up again. "Thank you for that thank you for not just walking by and leaving thanks for caring." BD grabbed Concretes head pulling him into a manly hug.

"I got you son." Concrete froze then pulled back. "I mean I'm just saying I know I'm not ya daddy I know how you feel about it I remember the conversation." BD corrected his self being fully genuine.

"Nah its cool…you cool."

"That means a lot to me. Cause I know how you get down." BD turned around quickly wiping his eyes before turning back. "This the chop shop and tonight you taking your first body." He handed a gun to him. "Moe will be here in about ten fifteen minutes he and I are going to chop it up. We suppose to finalizing a deal but really he finalizing his life he doesn't know I just learned he stealing from me. So his territory is about to be yours. Now he is going to feel real safe and secure cause he know it's just me and him tonight no goons."

"What about when he sees me?"

"His legacy will be lived through you he just don't know and won't expect it. You just stay away but close doing whatever you young people do and when I get done talking about left and right hands with a clap you shoot ya shot."

"Bet."

"Bet, Happy Birthday."

BD noticed the car of his questionable young team pulling up front.

"They pulling up." Stunna yelled as he open the garage door. "What up young ones yall pull up right on the dot don't cha? Just make it easy for a nigga to blow ya head off if they wanted to. Don't you lil niggas know being on time is actually being late and never be somewhere the exact time they expecting you, go early check the scene or go late catch they ass letting they guard down." Stunna was thoroughly disgusted. "I hope the pussy and that party was out of this world for the money yall lost." Stunna taunted them.

"Man Fatz fat ass was the one staying there last night he aint want to go to the party." Rell spitted out.

"So you the snitch in the family, tell it just like that huh" X chimed in poking his head out his car. "Nobody aint even ask a question yet and you throwing niggas under the bus. Yall watch too much First 48, that is not how you suppose to handle an integration. Those niggas is getting killed or beat up soon as them cameras leave." X was now standing in front of the car they sat in.

"X what I just told you bout theses young niggas, they spineless man."

"Nigga I got heart!" Fatz said opening the passenger car door sticking his feet out "Fuck you mean? Yall not just gone downplay me in my face like that. Us young niggas sit in that rat trap all day serve and collecting, it take a different type of breed to just play with yo own freedom like that. I mean yall niggas aint doing it."

"That's because we did our time" Concrete said coming down the stairs. "Look this aint about who got more heart this about who stole my shit and who let them do it."

"OG my bad no disrespect I aint know you was here but they was trying my hand."

"You are Fatz right?"

"Yeah, yep that's me. Damn you know my name."

"I know everybody that handles my money and merchandise. First things first though you telling me when I'm not around this is how you talk to my lieutenant and staff? You do understand when I'm not around they are me right." Con was in the backseat moving around a lot. Concrete lifted his gun "Get yall little asses out the car come stand over here in front of me. Sitting in the car like yall at the drive in and I'm a fucking movie. Sitting in the car like yall scared to move and shit. Don't yall want to know who stole from you? I really think you would Fatz since you all about being respected. Squirt!" Concrete stated not taking his eyes off Fatz.

"Yes sir."

"Tell me what you told X this morning." Squirt told his story word for word of his and X's earlier conversation. "Okay now Rell and Con what yall was fighting for today? Both of you weak as shit because aint nobody limping and aint shit wrong with ya faces but some scratches and dumb ass looks." Stunna giggled

"I told you a whole new breed they can't even fight."

"I'll beat ya ass."

"Said the Snitch Rell." Sunna taunted and laughed

"Yo short ass a whole hoe always waving that gun around you sure you not the part of this new breed pussy boy?" Stunna lifted his pistol.

"Stunna we interrogating these niggas we need em alive. Yall youngins got to understand there is order in a family and like all families you must respect your elders. See right now at this moment I'm like ya daddy. I can save you from an ass whooping but when he sees you later without my presence he might just beat or end your ass. Now what was the fight about?"

"Some hoes at the party last night. I was supposed to hook these girls to come with me and Con but instead the girls came with me. Then they threw him this real big back in the day Kelly Price shaped girl."

"Fuck you know about Kelly Price jitt?" X interrupted "My bad go ahead"

"She was real pretty though."

"Man that bitch was bigger than Fatz talking bout she was pretty though." Con finally spoke for the first time since being there "My little ass can't do nothing with no big ass girl like that. Plus you know I had been crushing on Cassie since forever. Man just thinking bout that shit make me want to beat yo ass." The emotion on Con face told Concrete these lil niggas was for real.

"Yall can roll around on the ground again as soon as we figure out who got our shit. Fighting over bitches yall out here getting money let them broads fight over you." X said growing agitated.

"Fatz why you didn't stay at the trap like you told them you would what you had to do that was so important?" Concrete asked folding his arms over his chest.

"My mom had called me." Everybody was silent then Concrete asked his next question.

"Why nobody told a higher chain of command what happened?"

"I might have been the person to find out first I went to the trap to relieve Fatz but nobody was there. I had two twenties on me I tryna get rid of when they was gone I went back to cook and get shit ready that's when I noticed everything was gone, went to look for the money it was gone too. It would be about a thirty minutes before X would come for the stuff so I figured Fatz hid it since he left. I called him he didn't answer so I went outside and started asking around anybody seen Fatz or have they seen anybody hanging round our trap. I didn't get anything from anybody everybody acting like they aint seen or heard nothing. Called Con him and Rell was arguing couldn't even get shit in while on the phone. X came while I was asking around that's why no one told yall they didn't know." Squirt was looking scared as shit "I'm sorry Concrete."

Concrete rubbed his chin yo think. "Okay. Fatz what did your momma want?"

"Um…She aint want shit."

"Then why did you leave."

"I told you my momma called me"

"But I thought she aint want shit."

"I didn't know that until I got to there. You know mommas." Squirt nudged Fatz as to say nigga is you crazy "Well you know what I mea…"

"Why you aint go back to the trap?" Concrete was losing his patience.

"I was tired look at me, I'm fat I aint about to do too much walking."

"You know the trap is never closed when there is product on the scene right?"

"Yea of course I been working for you along time I know the rules."

"Squirt where did they break into the trap at?"

"Nothing was broken or kicked in."

"So which door or window was left open?"

"I used my key to get in, nothing was open our windows nailed shut."

"So the thief is right before my eyes."

"I bet it's the nigga with all that heart." Stunna said

"I agree, cased closed" X chimed in

"Fellas a nigga with heart gone own up to that shit. If he did it at least let him tell us why or if we looking at the wrong guy."

"I got heart but I aint stupid naw OG I ain't do that shit I vouch for me and Con we was together all fucking night long shit everybody know we never leave each other side." Rell said fear in his eyes.

"They also know we aint dumb enough to steal from you lock the door then go home." Con said speaking for the second time of the night.

"I aint do it. That's all Ima say about that." Squirt stated Concrete X and Stunna all looked at Fatz.

"So Mr. Heart what's your story and before you say anything we know you did it. X knew when he seen you earlier at your moms. I know because of your tone. Concrete he's more of a logics man, all arrows point to you."

"I told yall man plus yall aint hurting off that litt…" Before Fatz could finish the word little Concrete had shot him in the dome one kill shot looking over to the other three.

"Are we going to have a problem like this again fellas?" They shook their heads no looking Concrete in the eyes hoping he believed them. "Anybody want out the game?" Concrete taunted them "You better speak now or forever hold your peace." They stood frozen in fear scared to make the wrong move. "Good I'm glad we had this conversation fellas. I'll see who I have around to take Fatz place until then it's just yall three Stooges. On top of that I need two of yall on lookout duty and one runner yall do that for three days then yall can go back to making some money." Concrete turned walking back up to his office. The boys just stood there Squirt watched Concrete while con and Rell looked at Fatz X took em out they thoughts.

"Check his pockets take all that jewelry off then strip him naked. Put all his shit in this trash bag. X gone hike his truck up with the pulley, slide them floor doors open then push him down that hole on the floor." They did exactly what Stunna said no one said anything until the splash from the body hit a body of water.

"What's down there?" Squirt said

"Yo last destination if one of you niggas ever cross me." Concrete said from the top of the staircase. "Hundreds of unfed piranhas" The three young men listened to what sounded like a steady rain fall for about ten minutes.

"Well look like the show is over. Yall know ya new assignments get to it." Stunna taunted them as they made their way to their car.

Chapter five

BD knew about Concrete because he knew his parents he actually went to school with them, and at one point he could have Concretes daddy. He lost that challenge. He would watch Shonda Concrete's mother here and there from afar and only spoke when he dared. Many times Concrete was right there while trying to talk to his mother so when he seen him at the dumpster he knew exactly who he was.

He knew about the death of Concretes parents which really fucked with him personally for a couple months after. That death was highlighted all over counties. Asking and pleading for help on solving the Tampa Bay area vicious double murder slash home invasion with one survivor that led to no arrest. It took the police one full hour to make it to the scene after a tip was called in from a child. He was aware that this was the child who witnessed some heartless being in one night snatched his whole childhood from him in one clean sweep at a still fairly pure age. So when he seen him he wouldn't let a little solider die or be broken from the pain of a half evil world. He couldn't adopt him so he did what he could he took him under his wing and recruited him.

His love for Shonda couldn't allow him to just walk past jitt. Way back when after he lost Shonda to Concretes dad he became the ultimate player. He made his self to believe no one woman could ever hold him down. He was no longer Derek but BD now "Big Daddy the Ladies Man". He had his main lady but whenever she turned her back one of back in the day devotes would be there waiting wanting and willing to play Mrs. BD for a couple of hours if not the whole night. With that being said he would probably never have children being that he could not see himself settle and really happy with just one women in the near future. So when he saw Concrete he saw a chance to raise, build, mold, and mentor a son. The fact that he was the blood of his first and only true love made the effort that much easier.

Concrete was tired after handling the loose ends with the boys. He Stunna and Tommy did a light turn up they went to the strip club where Tommy and Stunna both ordered Steak and fries with a bottle of Rose. Concrete couldn't understand how someone ate and let somebody be all around they food butt bootyhole naked, shit was weird. He couldn't wait to be home. Tommy was right about what he said earlier that day; about how he didn't see these women he craved his Niecy. And want to shame them at the same time. He couldn't get home fast enough.

Concrete watched over Niecy as she slept he wanted to wake her but since she was pregnant a lot of privileges she didn't hold before she now owned and he actually wanted to shower her with them. She was a good woman.

"Baby I feel you looking at me." Niecy moaned.

"I wasn't looking at you I just walked in."

"Yea bout ten minutes ago."

"This baby, even though it's small don't let me sleep." Niecy sat up placing two pillows behind her back. "And you know how I love my sleep. I have been up." She extended her arms for him to come lay on her lap. "How was your day today? I wasn't expecting you so early I figured yall would be parting all throughout the night for X birthday." Concrete laid his head snugged in Niecy lap eyes closed with his arms wrapped around her as if she were his pillow.

"It was a long day. I had to act like crazy ass Pablo Escobar today remind mother fuckers that I'm a little off."

"You're not off just cautious and determined two things that can make you appear to be crazy."

"You and X are the only people that understand me."

"God knew what he was doing when he put us in each other lives all those years ago."

"He defiantly blessed me when he put you there"

"I think I was the one that was being blessed. You are home now so just relax let me rub your back."

Concrete drifted as thoughts of childhood float through his mind. He knew Niecy from when his parents were still alive she grew up in the same hood which was like a housing complex. They were just cool right off the bat they just clicked ever since the first time they met. Their parents were hella different from each other but they clicked together too. They never had the whole boyfriend girlfriend vibe just the cool as fuck vibe. She could hold conversation without being all weird. She could talk basketball. She could do flips. She hulked big ass loogies and always held her own she wasn't scary. To put the icing on the cake she wasn't no busted looking dog she was a sight to see.

They were like sister and brother. She kept the girls in check on both of their ends and he did the same with the boys. As they got older they drifted for about two years by the age of sixteen they were barely keeping in contact with one another he was tryna get to the bag and figured she was too school wise. BD trusted Concrete so much that he had a lot to take care of he didn't really have time to be social he was basically running shit. Somewhere in their absence from each other Niecy got side tracked. He heard she wasn't into ball anymore and her grades were dropping along with her swerving her home girls. Concrete also knew she had a little dude or whatever that had been checking for her because the guy came and asked him about her. He just told him you fuck with her you fucking with me and left it at that he knew Niecy was sharp as a needle. All that she losing her shit just made him laugh like yeah right not his dawg she knew better. They was both getting older and the older you get the more your priorities shift with you. Hell he figured she was somewhere laying under some lame she could boss around. With all the money and moves he was making he finally got his first taste of some pussy matter fact it was a double shot two bad bitches on the first time. His now business partner was actually the bi girl who brought her girl and they both popped his cherry. How he seen it if women got a rush like men did he understood her dilemma and confusion in life at that time sometimes you just want to have fun.

One summer night he was going out it was a celebration he would be seventeen in less than twenty four hours. It was him Tommie and Stunna they had decided to go out to Club XS in route Stunna got a call it was a one hundred hit. They detoured and pulled up to the spot by a bodega where the chick flashed her cell phone to give her location. Stunna hoped out the car over to her "Here hurry up." Walking back to the car Stunna stopped dead in his tracks.

"Aye bitch you short twenty dollars." Another voice in the shadows spoke out.

"See bitch I told you all them one dollar bills wasn't gone do nothing."

"Who back there?" Stunna shouted looking spooked.

"It really doesn't matter. That fifty dollar bill mine so give me mine. I don't got shit to do with her games."

"Yes you do because you let her try and play." Stunna said getting agitated that he was speaking to someone in a dark alley. "Man who is that back there?"

"That's my friend don't worry about her that is her fifty though." The jay Denna said finally addressing Stunna's question.

"You hoes done lost yall mind?"

"Denise, damn Stunt her name Denise shit now what you gone give us our shit?"

"You said it her money so it would be her shit. I don't know no fucking Denise is this fucking set up bitch?"

"Just give her my fucking fifty and go." The voice yelled from behind the shadows clearly about to lose her shit.

"Bitch I weighed it for a bill, who the fuck you think you talking to? Talking all that shit backed up in the dark, show ya face fucking base head."

"Give a base head respect they putting food on ya plate." That's all Concrete needed to hear to know who behind the shadows and stop him from beating the shit or make shorty behind the shadows suck his dick.

"Yea you heard what the fuck she said we feed you nigga put some respect on our name." The old crack head started to turn up. Right when Stunna was raising his hand Concrete called out shutting the car door behind him as he stepped closer to Stunna. "Get yo ass in the car nigga."

"What nigga?"

"Get yo ass in the car." They squared up for second then Stunna began laughing.

"Consider that your birthday gift." Stunna said walking to the car. Concrete threw two crisp hundred dollar bills through the window.

"Thank you for the gift bro. Yall go on ahead all yall bickering brought something to my attention that I need to handle." After they pulled off Concrete turned to face his demons.

"Um cuse me sir but he just let with our dope and money."

"Well I guess this a night for you to get your life in order."

"Or I can suck your dick for something look I don't have any teeth." Denna opened her mouth to show her grill

"Get the fuck out of here bitch before you not have a tongue either. I will snatch that bitch just for the disrespect."

"Disrespect really you just stole from us. You owe me and my home girl back there." Oh yeah home girl back there Concrete thought turning to address the girl in the shadowed alley.

"Blood, don't shake em too bad."

"Blood? She aint no mother fucking blood, wait you like em young. You could tell by that slick ass mouth she got huh. I mean she might like you, you kind of cute..."

"Bitch do you have a death wish?" Concrete pulled out his pistol from his back and shot grazing her ear.

"Mother fucka got damnit!" Denna was holding her head. "I'm bleeding."

"Next time you want be so lucky. Give me a reason." Denna stepped back looking in the dark past Concrete while pressing her ear.

"You on yo own baby girl, you know where I be at. Crazy cute ass nigga the cute ones always the craziest." Denna sprinted off down the block.

After that night he had never let Niecy out of his sight. He was just happy to have her part of his life for damn near most of it. She was his best friend shelter and lover. He erased the bad and evil he had done today with every stroke she ran down his back.

"Daniel!!"

"Yes baby?"

"I been sitting here talking to you and just been ignoring me. What you were thinking about?"

"I was thinking bout you" Concrete turned over facing Niecy

"Yea okay tell me anything. Daniel just remember the day is over and tomorrow is brand new, but one thing for certain two things for sure that will never change is me and my love for you." She kissed him on his forehead.

"My forever friend."

"You damn right, now get yo heavy head ass off me. Ignoring me like you can't hear, and turn off them lights."

"Forever my lady it's like a dreeeaa..."Niecy hit him with a pillow and laughed.

"Shut up and good night, that is not going to work tonight."

Chapter six

X called Stunna over to pass along what Concrete had told him about his move. Everything for him was already in motion from his new spot different whip new number and everything to accommodate his new role he would be taking on. He looked at Stunna who was lounging in his lazy boy flipping through his phone. He wondered if telling Stunna the news and role that he wanted him to play in it was ideal or not. He didn't know really if Stunna could handle it how he wanted him to. He knew Stunna handled his business and was about correcting any standing issues. It was just that he was hot head you just never knew the mood he was in or what could trigger him. He didn't have a in between. Moods and reactions were important because it was what put a lot of attention on people. He continued to watch him from the kitchen island. Stunna looked restless swinging his leg that hung over the chair. Either way Stunna was next up then a jitt he molded a couple years back would be up under Stunna those were the two niggas that would have to answer every one of his questions and better have had all the right ones too.

It was crazy how even though Stunna was the oldest that X still looked at the youngin Tariq as a much better candidate. Being that Stunna was older and a hot head if X even thought of putting jitt before Stunna in rank he would probably try and kill the little boy and then kill X. He loved the nigga and actually trusted him with his life but would never put shit past him to do that would be to call himself a fool. It was time to pass the information on, they would soon be working closer than ever before his true own confidant. X didn't like switching up constantly a little here and there but minor changes. Keeping the same circle kept you out of trouble. And telling only one person everything kept the confusion down on any leaks you'll always know who the rogue was.

"What up nigga. what you in yo phone studying you aint picked yo head in a minute?" X was feeling out his mood.

"Shit it's this bad bitch on the gram she call herself checking for a nigga. I'm trying to going through her pictures and friends list to see what she be on."

"Let me see her." Stunna lifted the phone leaning over for X to grab it then leaned back in his seat.

"Aye she bad aint she?"

"Damn yea shawty is bad a little thick black queen."

"Yea but I don't do them dark chicks. I need an exotic."

"Whatever nigga yo short ass need not, be too picky."

"What? Like Chris Brown say I like em with the good hair." Stunna was laughing so hard at his own joke X knew he was in good mood not to trip about the height comment.

"Concrete hooking me up with the connect." Stunna laugh cut off quick looked dead in in X's eyes while putting his phone in his lap and crossing his arms.

"Word?"

"Yep told me a few days ago" Stunna shifted in his seat

"You able to move like that?" X just raised a brow shrugging his shoulders. Stunna watched him while he rubbed his chin. "So you about to be the big man huh?"

Stunna stood up extending his hand to congratulate him pulling him in for a quick hug. "That what's up man, don't forget us little people bruh."

"Shit I can't you coming with me you definitely needed, you bout one of the only ones I trust beside Concrete."

"Say less, let's get this money."

Stunna was on cloud one hundred he was really bout to get in the game where he would be making some real moves and money now. X always looked out and fed him when he could. He had been trying to place him in good grace with Concrete by staying so close to him and Stunna recognized that. Stunna had felt tension between him and Concrete since his birthday night years ago. Stunna always felt like on that particular night Concrete tried him and let them jays get away with that bullshit. It was a principle thing. As of a couple minutes ago that shit no longer mattered that was old news right along with Concrete ass.

Stunna was wild boy same age a Concrete and X and extremely hungry for success. He was from Tampa where he lived with his parents who often took alternative shifts residing in the Hillsborough County jail. Until they finally both ended up in there together over some petty and felony charges. At the age of thirteen he moved with his grandparents on his mother side in Orlando who couldn't keep reigns on him so they gave guardianship over to his uncle on his Father side on the west side of Tampa. When he got back to Tampa he linked up with X kind of by accident and stuck by him from there on out. Stunna always felt like he was owed everything because he never really had nothing so when he made moves with X it just felt right. He knew all the robbing he was doing wasn't the lick it was more like just a good side hustle. It wasn't his niche slanging and strong arming was. Stunna was high yellow with fat locks he kept short and wild and slim but built like a youngin in his prime and was 5'1 feet tall he could get a lady but most looked over him literally. He always wanted to show his hand his power his strength over his manhood to take up for the size. He wanted money and power once he had that bitches would easily and willingly flock. It was finally time for him to set himself up like a king.

After a full day and night of tryna hustle information put some people in place and move some shit around for his own benefit Stunna decided to text Concrete.

X told me about your news. Congratulations to you and your wife on the baby! You making bigger moves I see. I just want to assure you everything will be taking care of and I got X back. You don't have to worry about anything. I have been watching and learning you two for years now. We got this.

Concrete open his phone to see a text from Stunna it made him uncomfortable. They never talked via phone or text always in person or through X. He shifted in his seat then replied.

Appreciate it!

He still didn't trust that nigga. He called his OG to take his mind of Stunna.

"YO!"

"BD what's up with you man?"

"Man out here where I be and doing what I do. You know it goes son. How is everything going your way?"

"Shit everything is everything filling shoes the best way I can."

"Yea them some big ass shoes I know because I wore them once."

"Thank you for passing them down."

"I would not have had any other way."

"Nine years of wearing then now they wearing thin."

"Only nine years."

"I got a good twenty three out of them."

"Yea well I could of beat you but I got some news."

"What is it?"

"I'm gone be a daddy."

"Congratulations! I was wondering how long after the court house marriage it would take."

"To be honest I wasn't expecting it all, I really think it surprised us both."

"Well she's a good loyal smart and beautiful woman the both of you deserve it."

"Thank you. Yea they wasn't lying when they said he who find a wife finds a good thing."

"Amen. Wish I could have found a good thing."

"I don't see how you never found a love I can't figure out why."

"Just because you love somebody don't make them for you."

"Sorry BD."

"It's all good. I gets mine you a witness to that."

"True."

"So how X been?"

"X is cool he ready I held him down like you held me."

"It's true a smooth transition. I want you and your lady to come visit me before she drop."

"Already in the making." Concrete was caught off guard but a knock at his door "Aye somebody at my door hold on."

"Nah just call me back, I was in the middle of getting mine. Do ya thang. I'll holla at you later son."

"Later."

Concrete always appreciated those calls with BD they made him feel human somebody he could relate to and actually understood all the pressure that on his shoulders. He really did feel like a father and that he actually cared. Concrete opened the door his smiled ripped from his face.

"How the fuck did you get past the concierge and who told you where I live?"

"Is Niecy here? Bitch fuck you mean is Niecy here? You aint hear shit I just asked you?"

"I don't got to talk to you nigga."

"Niecy bring yo narrow ass out here."

"Baby why you yell… Denna what yo doing here."

"You told a Jay where we live? Woman please don't tell me you fucking with that shit again and while you carrying my baby."

"No baby you know I work at the shelter some days. That's how I got in touch with Denna we bumped into each other about a week ago since that alley incident years ago. Plus she is recovering she's not using." Concrete sat his pistol on the coffee table

"Don't look like it, the truth is always in the eyes" Denna grimaced at the cold stare that he shot her way "What the fuck you want Denna?" he continued his stare.

"Baby cut it out please! What's up Denna you good?"

"Can we talk alone?"

"I hear see and pay everything up in here so try again."

"Baby! It's cool what's up Denna?" Niecy tried to console Denna motioning for Concrete put some space in between him and the girls she figured that may help her talk. Concrete moved over to the couch hoping this would help her hurry up and get the fuck out his space so he sat on the far end of the sofa and started messing through his phone. Niecy smiled and mouthed thank you.

"Go ahead Denna what's up?"

"Well I don't know what's going on but Stunna is over at the crack house calling himself delivering messages."

"Recovered huh? Yeah okay."

"D shut up damn."

"He make a bitch not even want to give you a heads up. Yo nigga so fucking ignorant yo." Denna was shaking her head with a side eye. Concrete winced at the sight of judgmental eyes and a baser calling him ignorant addressing him lesser than herself.

"Denna I'm tired, what is it that you need to tell me?"

"Stunna over there talking bout he about to be the distributor of the city the big man. He sayin soon everybody will be bowing down when they see him begging to eat. Talking bout he will soon hold the keys to the drug game and take out any and everybody in his way. I think he's high or some shit I don't know. I have seen him kill before I know what death in eyes look like." Denna looked over at Concrete who was still playing around on his phone feet kicked up on the table in front of him. She turned back to Niecy and continued. "I know that nigga doing his thing but he aint shit. Everybody know it's yo nigga or at least they think it's him who running these streets so when I heard him talking about taking niggas out I figured you was in danger. When he left I did too and came right over. I was about to get high for the second time today but you came before that. I couldn't forget about you to give you the heads up." Concrete heard everything and thought how he could hurt this nigga before he even tried to make any stupid moves.

"Thank you Denna I really appreciate you telling me this, it means a lot. You have been looking out since the first day of meeting you my lil street momma."

"I aint nobody momma." Niecy pulled her out of her seat giving her a hug walking her towards the door Niecy pulled a fifty dollar bill from her pocket and slipped it in her hand. "Be careful Denna." Niecy shut the door turning to look at Concrete who was no longer on his phone but looking at her.

"Go pack us a bag."

"Okay."

Concrete sat and thought this nigga just texted me. He had to fix this now the sooner the better. "Niecy put one of them burner phones and that piece of paper in the jewelry box that says Coolio with the number on it in the bag too." Stunna didn't know where he lived but that aggy crack head bitch Denna did and it was apparent they didn't get along so for the right price Stunna could easily get their location.

CONCRETE

Chapter seven

Niecy hated when Concrete left to handle business at night. She didn't feel in danger or anything like that she was in well-known territory at her grandma and grandpa's in their guest house. With what Denna told her she just wanted her man beside her or at least for him to be in her vicinity. Now she really understood why Concrete never talked in front or to her about his lifestyle because just the little piece she got was making her worry like hell. Like were there people who he really considered his friend really out their cursing him with death it was a terrible thing for her to think of. The fact that this was his lifestyle the reason he woke up every morning to put up with envy. Envy jealousy those were deadly traits they cause hate. She could not lose her man to this. She would have to pray more and keep doing her being his friend and motivation. The things she was good at.

It was 2:06 am she knew he was smart and handling himself. He loved the night time and at one time she actually got why he wanted to be out exploring at night. Even though she enjoyed the night life in her rebel days she never forgot what Concretes dad said.

Niecy thought about how back in the day they knew when the sky turned orange it was time to go in mainly because it was around nine pm. Low-key just like Concrete Niecy hated that shit too having to be inside early but hearing the kids outside still running and playing. Her parents told it was because they didn't have anybody to care for them. She said her and Concrete were lucky and would understand later on down the road when no pass troubles or issues came back knocking on their doors. As Niecy got older she ended up chillin on the porch while it was dark never leaving the porch though just out being a part of the nighttime. Then she slowly made her way over to her friends' houses during the night for like little sleep overs to all out just sneaking out because the night time just made her feel so alive. Her mind worked best at night. She seemed to the most alert and creative.

They were about six or seven when they started craving being outside later.

"Man why we can't just sit on the porch when it gets dark. It aint like we got school or nothing else to do." Concrete pouted.

"I know right but you know at night is when most of the bad stuff happen."

"Bad stuff happen all day everyday round here"

"True but most of the time grown folks know what they talking about."

"Most of the time, not all."

"Whatever Daniel I'm about to go home because I don't want nothing bad happening to me tonight."

"Scary cat."

"Yo mammy."

"Yo greasy baldheaded granddaddy."

"Whatever see you tomorrow bruh." That's when Daniels dad stepped out

"This is the one you gone marry. She smarter than you and don't just listen and follow behind you. She got a mind of her own. Both of yall need to remember nothing is out at night but the devil his followers and his slave's point blank period."

Her thoughts made her drift to sleep dreaming of her in Concrete living a normal drugless lifestyle with no neighbors and a shit load of kids. Dreaming about all them bad ass kids is what made her wake up. She woke up to see Concrete sleeping on the couch she didn't even car he wasn't in the bed she was happy he was just home. She tipped toed back to the room so he wouldn't wake up he needed the rest. The last few days had been busier than usual and reminded of just how much of a reality that her man was a drug dealer in real life.

Rinng rinnng rinnng

So much for that attempt she thought shaking her head with a deep exhale she just decided to make her way to the kitchen. Concretes body shifted on the couch and then jumped up to alert state, he removed his phone from his pockets.

"Hello."

"It's a lizard infestation."

"Alright, I'm about to leave now."

"You want me heat you up something before you leave Daniel?"

"No I'm good baby. I'll be back as soon as I can."

"Okay be safe."

These last couple of days had made Concrete extremely happy about his exit plan. In all the years he had been working he aint never had days like these. First his own team was stealing from him. Then the homies homie want's to kill him, and know somebody was using the product and claiming revenge for Fatz. All of this in a weeks' time, he couldn't believe it. Concrete pulled up on X who was sitting at the park he parked his car then hoped in with X letting him give the learned details and navigate them to check the scene.

"So I guess what happened to Fatz has been way too much for some to handle. Come to find out after our meeting while Rell was supposed to be on duty being lookout he asked Toad to sell him some molly then came right back around a little later asking for crack. Come to find out he wasn't getting it off he been taking it. Guess this morning he was out in the road making a scene on the streets. Toad said he was asking folks have they seen Fatz then in the same breath telling them and won't see him anywhere either because he killed him. Fatz is gone and aint nothing anybody can do about it. Toad even said the police started coming around shortly after that asking about Fatz."

"Stunna did call him the snitch."

"I wonder where he at he would of murked the nigga off GP for that shit."

"Did yall take care of his phone all the shit out the shop right?"

"Nigga this is my life too."

"True."

X and Concrete sat found a nice spot a good distance from the corner Rell was working. He was missing in action for a minute then finally popped up.

"There he go right there."

"Yea that nigga high because he aint even notice us out here at all he was just a few feet from us."

"What is he doing?"

"He looking out, maybe he a little paranoid. Shit I would be too if I brought the police out."

"Shit you aint never lied. Yea, I guess you right I'm not used to seeing him pace like that. The shit makes him look nervous and since I'm already looking for him to be doing some crazy shit anyways it just threw me off a little."

"They said he was doing and talking a whole lot of shit earlier."

"Let's just watch him for a while."

"Okay." The two men watched him as he paced back and forth up the block looking at somethings slightly longer but nothing really out of the ordinary.

"But check him out though. How he doesn't even see us he don't know the whip and if he can't make the whip he see the lights. He aint even over here checking."

"Maybe he does see us and know exactly who we are."

"Naw he look like he tripping to me. Look at him that don't even look like Rell."

"Where Con at?"

"Con I think he working twenty second and Osborne."

"Let's go check on Con and see what he on." Pulling up to Osborne it was looking pretty slow but what they didn't expect to see on the Corner was Stunna and Con. Stunna looked like he was telling him some deep shit the way his hands and body moved he was telling a story and not just telling him something. "Pull over" Concrete said

"Already on it homie."

"Bet." With all the shit going on Concrete needed time just a second to talk to his baby check on her and see how she was holding up. He really never was away from her for whole full days like this. He looked over at X like who was looking like he couldn't believe what they pulled up on. With the day being so busy he hadn't made his personal runs so he took a second to text Niecy to go get some supplies.

He would just call her later to talk to her. Con noticed a car sitting a little ways up the street from them he just made a mental note. What Stunna was telling him was way more interesting that car.

"I just wanted to put something in your ear so yall could be hip. Get back to work lil nigga."
Con nodded at Stunna then put his eyes back on the car up the street while piecing the story Stunna had just given him together. So according to Stunna Concrete and X are thinking about killing him Rell and Squirt because they knew what really happened to Fatz. They don't trust them and really thought all four of them was in it together. Apparently this was the reason Rell was over in Tampa Park going crazy. Stunna relayed this message to him earlier this morning. It aint make sense to Con cause why would they kill three of their best trap workers they would be losing money. Plus they could have killed them all that night. It just didn't add up to him. Con started walking toward the car that had still not moved or had one passenger exit. The car lights came on and it reversed pulling off before Con could even get a good stride in.

"So did that look suspect or like Stunna was handling business."

"I don't even know the shit looked weird. What the fuck he got to say to them kids especially Con that nigga barely ever opens his mouth so what kind of business they got."

"Apparently some silent business."

"Apparently" They both laughed at the pun.
Concrete and X decided to stop and eat neither of them remember the last time they had a meal. They pulled up to firehouse deciding on some good food and drink and a block

space of no work could get them back into full gear. Before even getting a good distance from the car a group of young boys approached them. Concrete now wished he had parked in the front instead of round back in the dark.

"What's up OG 'S?"

"Tryna eat."

"Aint we all" who appeared to be the little leader started "I know you. Are you Concrete?"

"Yea why?" Concrete had his hand on his gun handle in the small of his back. A well put together boy came from the back and looked at Concrete.

"My cousin work for you, have you seen him?"

"Who?"

"Didn't yall house get hit the other day?"

"No" X answered

"You are lying. Aye these nigga's is soft yo shit missing nobody head been blown off you aint hung a body next to the shoes on them electricity wires. What's up, why are yall lying?"

"No what's up with yall we just trying to eat."

"Why yall lying ignoring the question? We know yall did something he been missing for days and his fat ass love his momma cooking. All of a sudden it he aint around on top of that his homeboy talking bout aint nobody gone ever see him again. Who says things like that bout they friend."

"Well what the fuck do that have to do with us maybe his fat ass got a girl that can cook better."

"Look we know you did something that's our cousin just like we know yall got robbed. When Fatz eat he goes into a comma afterwards. We made a copy of his key way back when. Him leaving the trap, we set that up. Got auntie to call his phone, we needed something that would divert him from the house. He can't say no to his moms. And just like that we eating off yo table, getting full."

"Is that so?"

"Shole is would of got away with it too if his dumb ass didn't lock the door behind us when we left fucking stupid." The boy said tapping another young man next to him in the back of the head.

"So what yall coming to bring us our things back?"

"More like here so you can tell us were our cousin a?t"

"Looks like you all killed him."

"Well it look like we got a motha fucken problem."

"Yea you got that right but it's not our problem." Following the rules left handle left right handle right and work your way from the outside in. Two men handling two guns with four young men to take care of, piece of cake. The quartet were all dead before they could try and bust another note.

"I done lost my appetite lets go see bout Rell then eat. Maybe these niggas was the reason he tripping." Concrete and X pulled up to Rill's block to see him chillin on a wall looking more like himself. Concrete whistled and Rell came strolling over.

"What up Rell you good?"

"I just had some bad Molly the other day that what all that was about."

"All of what about?" Concrete acted confused. Rell was surprised he asked then answered.

"I was worried yall was gone kill the rest of us three since yall thought we was in cahoots and shit. But the truth is out so I'm not even worried bout that."

"Who told you I was gone kill you?"

"Stunna, but word on the street Fatz didn't do it."

"We know we handled it."

"But my brother by affiliation is dead. Don't you realize yall killed that nigga for nothing?"

"You was there we all heard the facts. You seen the nigga acting like shit was sweet he held no remorse."

"Fuck! Fuck yall. Yall niggas aint shit you don't deserve to be here, since we as people can just decide. Somebody needs to take your life."

"Are you threating me? What you wanna do you wanna be where Fatz at?"

"Fuck you!"

"I suggest you get to your spot where you belong. Do you want someone else to die just because right here right now you not doing what you supposed to be doing, looking out?"

Rell walked off in a huff you can tell he was mad but they knew he wasn't gone do shit.

"Concrete you think we gone have to pop one of these young niggas?"

"Naw they just letting steam off this they first go round where someone died and they made a choice to kind of they guilty. It will brush over they not gone say shit out of pure guilt. Speaking of guilt that's what I feel for not talking or checking in with my baby all day let me call her real quick."

"Handle ya business we all know she run shit." They both laughed as he dialed Niecy's phone. When she picked up he felt a surge or peace flow through him.

"Niecy hey baby how you doing?"

"I'm good Daniel how about you?"

"Better now. Did you get everything I texted you?"

"Yeah I got it I'm walking from the register as we speak. I'm on my way back to Grandmas where I will finish the task."

"Cool. Alright baby drive safe I'll see you when I get over there."

"Okay talk to you later."

Niecy hung up happy to finally hear Concrete's voice. She didn't know what was going on she really didn't care because she felt safe and trust concrete she was his ride or die she would always hold him down because he always rode for her. On her walk to the car she inhaled and rubbed her little belly she realized she was hungry and didn't eat much today. When she went to open the door she noticed she didn't have her keys in hand probably because she was so focused on what Concrete had to say. So she stopped to look through her purse then walked towards the front of the car to place her bags down on the hood to search her purse. A humming car sound made her look up to see a big something speeding her way causing her to jump on the hood of the car in time to avoid being hit but the side swipe impact of her car jolted her off and to the front left side of her vehicle. She looked up catching a glace of a tail light cutting a corner. She grabbed her purse and the contents of the bags she carried from the ground.

"OH my God are you okay Miss." A lady yelled running towards her

"What happened?" another voice urged

"Someone just tried to hit her."

"Did anybody get a make or the license plates?" a man called out.

Somebody just tried to hit me! Niecy thought to herself. Luckily for her she always had quick reflexes, she owed that to sports. "You move quick girl." the lady that ran to help said. Niecy hate being called girl "Your car didn't have such luck. Bastard took your side rearview and fucked up your paint decent." She said looking at Niecy car. "You should take pictures for your insurance."

"I'm glad I won't have to use any health insurance that's for damn sure." Niecy said with a slight smile.

"Who was it some crazy ex?"

"That I can assure it wasn't been with the same man for years and he's going to be livid."

"As he should. Want me to stick around while you wait on the police? I'm sure somebodies called it in."

"I just want to go back inside for a minute."

"I can walk you in."

"It's fine I got it from here."

"Shoot yourself, you be careful young lady."

"Thank you for your help." Niecy took a moment to take everything in and just let her body calm down before she headed back inside the store. Since she was a regular customer who was loyal and spent top dollar she asked to go through back terminal of the shopping plaza. They were cool with it. She ordered an Uber who arrived four minutes later and she slid out the back door and into the back seat slouching down in route to her grandmother's house.

In the house when she got situated and immediately reached out to Concrete to let him know what happened.

"Daniel somebody just tried to hit me."

"Don't be trying to fight these folks out here with my baby inside you."

"No somebody just tried to run me over."

"Where you at you should have been home? That's what you get for making snack stops. Hurry up and get off the road Florida like to take everybody insurance high as fuck no matter who really at fault."

"Baby listen to me I was walking to my car and somebody in a truck literally tried to run my ass over. Like Big Red did the manager dude in five heartbeats."

"WHAT!?" Niecy felt his rage and that scared her "What donyou mean somebody just tried to run you over?"

"It all happened so fast I didn't see the car color or nothing but I know it was a dark color. I don't even know how I knew to jump something just told me move."

"What the fuck!' She heard Concrete hit something then she heard X voice say something. "Look, its ok don't worry I got you just, where are you now?"

"I'm at grandma house."

"Stay there."

"I will. I left my car at the plaza."

"It's okay I'll worry about that. Just go ahead and handle what you set out to do tonight then get some rest. Everything else let me handle. From here on out we good, you are good everything will be alright I got you and nothing will ever happen to you. Just remember you are my forever friend."

"I love you baby."

"I love you too."

"Hurry up and get over here so I can show you how much."

"Don't do that to me right now I'm trying to concentrate call you back in a few."

Niecy hung up and set everything up and began typing when she was done Niecy folded the letter and list and stuffed them in an envelope that had X on it and stored the envelope in a plastic Ziploc freezer bag. She pushed back from the desk throwing the typewriter the package of printing paper the hand written letter she just duplicated all into a black trash bag. After reaching the fire pit she started earlier threw the bag in it along with her gloves. She grabbed her poking stick then went and sat in a chair a few feet away from the fire watching it burn.

Deep in thought she went back to when she was a child. She remembered the day like it was yesterday. She was pissed walking down her street she had death on her mind. She heard people greeting her *"Hey Niecy!" "Niecy where you going girl?" "You alright?"* She didn't want to stop she didn't care to be nice and chit chat like her normal self she just wanted to talk to one person. When she reached the basketball courts she walked to the middle on the side lines looking among the players short tall old and young until she found who she was searching for.

"Daniel! Hey Daniel come here." She heard the kids taunting and making fun of him *"Oh your girlfriend calling?" "What you do Daniel." "Um, I think somebody bout to get dumped."* Daniel didn't respond he just ignored them while approaching her.

"What's wrong woman" He said when close enough. She grabbed his arm walking away from the court.

"That fat ass nigga Red, you know my cousin a Blood so Ima wanna be Blood Red."

"Yea"

"That nigga came to my house asking for flour for his momma and when I let him in. He said I seen yo people leave then his fat ass just jumped on me."

"What?"

"So we in the house fighting rolling around and shit. He ripped my shirt. Look" She showed him the ripped shirt she was wearing beneath the shirt she covered herself with. Daniels eyes got big

"He raped you or something?"

"No but he was trying to do something he had me scared for a minute I didn't know what to do. I stuck my thumb in his eye then his fat ass punched me in the chin and got up and left."

"Okay." Concrete started walking off.

"Daniel!"

"What?!" His tone scared her and shocked her. She was confused, probably would have cried if all them niggas and girls wasn't all around her.

"Nothing…never mind."

"Good now go home I'll see you later." Niecy couldn't believe Concrete just dismissed her like that. He was supposed to be her brother and he didn't even care that a nigga just violated her. He just went back to his stupid ass game. Like she said that's why my basketball team won last night. Niecy went back home cleaning and straightening everything that has been knocked and bumped during her little altercation earlier after that she went to the window to see what was happening outside which was nothing really until she spotted Red sitting outside with his friends. They were clowning him because of his face. They didn't believe he fell and hit the corner of the coffee table. She got mad just looking at him. She went upstairs and bathed once she hit the bed sleep covered her. She remembered waking up at about three in the morning to police sirens and seeing Daniel on her floor looking up at her. "I got you blood you are my forever friend" he rolled over. Niecy jumped out the bed and ran across the hall to the bathroom to the window opening it to peep the scene. Reds mother was crying in her neighbor's arms. Somebody tried to beat my baby to death.

"It's this house right here. I'll be right back X it'll only be a minute." As quick as Concrete went in he came out. "We going to 5977 Banche Drive."

X speed off reaching their destination 5 minutes quicker than the fifteen minute drive.

"That's the truck right there. There aint no lights on and it say he live alone."

"Say no more. She aint my Lady but that's my bitch."

Getting into the house was nothing they split up looking around until X found a frail young boy tapped out in fetal position in his boxers. Concrete slapped him in the back of his head waking him up.

"Good morning"

"What the…who the fuck is yall" the boy said reaching for his pants.

"You looking for this?" X waved his twenty two in front of him.

"Man aint no dope here, this where I live Ion got shit here. I got about seven thousand in that shoebox over there." X went and grabbed the shoe box looking in.

"Well we know he aint a liar." X took the bills and folded two stacks sticking them in his pocket.

"Really X"

"What? A dead man can't spend money."

"We aint killing him." X shrugged his shoulders

"Okay if you say so."

"The lady you tried to hit earlier" Concrete started it off "Why did you do it."

"Cause I was bored." Concrete pistol whipped him on each side of his face

"Fuck you nigga" This time he hit him in the nose with the butt of his gun."

"Why you do it?" The boy looked around his room then spit out blood "I just want answers I already did more than I wanted to." He wiped his nose screeching from the pain of just barely touching it. He knew it was broken.

"Ten grand"

"Somebody was gone pay you ten g's to do a hit and run?"

"Naw my nigga to kill her. You see that big ass truck outside. I was gone mush her ass." Concrete hand tightens on his gun.

"So why you didn't finish it?"

"That bitch was fast jumping up on shit like she cat woman. If she is pregnant she aint move like it. It was too many people around to go back. She never left out of there at least not in her car so I was gone run it back tomorrow and try my luck."

"Who ordered the hit?" the boy shook his head "I don't have beef with you. You were just the middle man I want the head."

"Stunna" The boys eyes closed as his head flew back and his lifeless body fell to the bed

"Damn I sorry dawg." X said to Concrete

Chapter eight

"Sup son heard you got some action going on out there."

"It's been a hell of a lot of movement."

"What's up you need me to come up or send some reinforcements in?"

"Nope everything bout taken care of to be completely honest. You know me I'm always one step ahead of the game."

"That's why I choose you because you don't get to into your feelings you always cool calm and collected. I mean always have been."

"Yea well I aint been to cool here lately but Ima handle it."

"I know you will. I'm just checking on you making sure you still floating."

"Fuck floating I'm gliding."

"It's true! Well if you need me you know the number. Go handle yo business jitt."

"That's all I can do."

"Peace."

See what most people didn't know is that when BD left and passed everything down to Concrete it wasn't just blocks or a little bit of the county. It was everything the whole Central and Northern part of Florida he distributed to. People were dabbing and chopping up with this man every day and no one ever knew he was filling they plates. At one point BD the local celebrity with just enough clout was that nigga. The nigga Creep that everybody knew by name but not by face he was that nigga. A time comes when you just got or want to let something go and when he made his number he passed that gigantic role to Concrete.

The day he sat in the barbeque joint and spoke to Concrete he knew right then and there who he would pass the torch to. BD didn't have a right hand he had workers and when Concrete came into the picture it was then that he had a son that he could mold. Now it was Concrete turn to pass the torch and tell X the only secret he had ever kept from him. X would now hold the Creep title pressure and responsibility. It would all be explained in a letter

It was exactly three days before X would be the big man of the city making big moves getting major money and loving the top crop of the ladies. Neither X nor Stunna knew shit was about to change big time for the both of them. All three of them had just finished their meal. Concrete wanted to celebrate and get any unfinished business handled and taken care of.

"Man fellas it has been a journey it started as two and ended as three only for time to repeat itself and take it back to two." Concrete extended his hands." I wish you brothers nothing but the best of luck man. Damn I can't believe I got a baby on the way I aint never even held a baby before. I can't bring jitt into this shit. I refuse to let him lose his parents like I lost mine. I have to live for my son and nobody else. My son Damn…I can't believe I'm saying that."

"I can you love that girl." X laughed

"Yea remember how you two met back up? Her fine ass was about to be chocking that night." Stunna said grabbing his dick. X shot him a look then looked at Concrete who was clinching his teeth.

"Watch ya mouth before I dig in it." Concrete said sliding his hand onto his gun. Everybody got quite X watched them both as they stared each other down the intense silence lingered forever. "Nah I'm just playin I remember." Releasing his pistol and placing his hands back on the table. "He works in mysterious ways that's for sure."

"Yea" Stunna piped in with a smile Concrete grimaced again.

"Speaking of..." he leaned in over the table which caused X and Stunna to mirror his actions off of impulse. "Look, the connect coming in two days early. He here today I guess a man with his weight wanted to move in early and keep em guessing. So X since you gotta go handle that in Fort Myers tomorrow you still go handle that and Ima send ya boy Stunna here to meet him in your place." X leaned back in his seat shocked while Stunna knocked the table lightly with his fist and a smile spreading across his face.

"What" X said calm with slight confusion and disbelief apparent on his face.

"It's cool X man I..."

"Shut the fuck up. What you mean meet him in my place? Once he met Stunna he aint fucking with me or nobody else you know that."

"No be cool it's cool X, trust me."

"Yea trust him." Stunna was leaning hard in his chair with his drink in hand pinky up making a cheers movement

"I said shut the fuck up." X said never taking his eyes off Concrete. "Now you know just like I know aint no trust in this game. Shit change constantly in this shit because you can't trust anybody. You send him and my chance is gone. I done set up all kind of shit for this move right here bro" X banged his hand on the table. "And you talking bout trust you."

"I promise what you have done it's not in vain, trust me."

"Trust you yeah okay, we gone see." X stood up throwing on his suit jacket that rested behind his chair finally looking over to Stunna who was still leaning and smirking X buttoned up his jacket. "So Stunt you got me big dawg?" Stunna lifted his hands as to surrender.

"Yo it's a sit in you still the big dawg, and yea you know I got ya." X walked off leaving Concreate and Stunna to talk.

X was irate his A1 day one just played him for a nigga he only tolerated and truly wanted to kill. Deep down he trusted Concrete but his brain and years of duty on the streets told him a different outcome. Distributors don't like their face and name known by too many people that caused for too many problems. How the fuck was someone supposed to just ride with this shit and trust him. They both knew better. X clinched the steering wheel then took off on 75S he would just get to Fort Myers a little early for some rest and relaxation.

"Okay so you good, you know everything you have to do right no fuck ups." Concrete quizzed Stunna

"I got it man listen this is something that you won't regret."

"Better hope not. My day one is pissed right now with the right to be. Shit he probably committing bodily harm to someone as we speak."

"He will be alright." Stunna said under his breath.

"Yea he will, I agree just let all this blow over and we'll be back to normal." Concrete stood buttoning he suit jacket "Since you the big dawg now how about you handle my tab too." Before walking off he stopped and turned. "Yo handle this make us proud. It was nice knowing you big dawg."

"Shit you leaving tonight?"

"Nah I'm just saying my goodbyes."

Stunna would have picked up everybody in the restaurant tab the way he was feeling. He spoke this shit into existence as far as he was concerned. He believed and knew he would be a boss to the highest extent one day. The fact that it actually happened without him having to do any dirty work made him believe it was even more so rightfully his. He had already got the location of where Concrete lived from this crack head Denna. He knew they were in a condo him and his girl right downtown. The nigga had been right up under his nose the whole time in an area that he frequented when he was bar hopping. He got work off on the white folks that were functioning crack heads they paid top dollar. He figured Denna would probably know were Niecy was and wherever Niecy was Concrete would be right behind on the side or on top. When he found out Denna didn't know he befriended her with extra dope telling her that she volunteered at the shelter and try and get in with her. After three months of tricking dope and being a little too nice for his taste Niecy finally gave him the information he requested about a week ago. Stunna had planned on taking Concrete out whenever he got close to the distributer through X. His plan was to get X to make him a partner so they handled all business together then after meeting the connect Knock X off and get to Concrete before he could avenge X's death. Now none of this plan had to happen because he won he was going to come out on top with no blood on his hands.

Stunna was behind the attempt hit and run. Stunna got Concrete address from his snitch Denna he went to handle them both early in the morning but no sight of them going in or coming out. He had figured Concrete would be steps ahead being close to his departure date from the hood. When he made eyes on Denise that young crack head who actually wanted to be saved he took his chance with the hit and run. He had never seen her but when he seen a picture of her he could see why concrete went to her rescue that night she was rare.

Even though he got what he wanted with no blood or tears shed. He knew in reality in the back of his head aint no way X could meet the plug without him or even if the plug even go for this plan Concrete had. The thing that made him doubt the street code is Stunna didn't know Concrete's reach he was so smooth what if someone was actually breaking the street ethics for him just this one time. In his eyes with the key in his hands he had to get rid of X and Concrete. He was going to get rid of Concrete first because he had the blueprint. X could be handled later.

Stunna pulled up to the spot thirty minutes earlier then when he was due to be there. Normally he would do this to pick out the scene but today he did it out of pure excitement. The meeting location was in Carrollwood at some housing community which kind of threw him off but he said fuck it. This is a whole new breed he fucking with they do different things. It was nothing but your regular white people shit going on nothing weird for them people jogging with the dog or alone. Talking in front of yards he even saw one white lady sunbathing between the houses in her back yard. Must be nice he mumbled. It was ten minutes to two pm he stepped out the car in his business suit walking around to the back of the car popping the trunk to retrieve a MCM duffle bag he closed the trunk continuing to the passenger side of the car where he grabbed a Publix shopping bag from the seat that was filled with snacks and drinks. He shut the door proceeding up the walkway then rang the doorbell. A Chico looking man peeped out the window next to the door and then disappeared seconds later he opened the door. He was tall and muscular with a look of try something I dare ya. Standing over Stunna with his stare he asked in a deep Mexican accent "What your name?"

"It's the numba one Stunna yep yep yep!" Stunna said doing a head bob Chico just looked at him blankly shifting in his stance. "Stunna. My name is Stunna."

"Come in." Chico stuck his head out the door looking both ways down the street then straight ahead before shutting the door. "Drop that shit" Stunna put both his bags on the floor along the side of him. Chico started to search him pulling his nine millimeter from his band and his revolver from his ankle. "You go to war?"

"You never know."

"I give back when you leave." Chico sat both guns on a table stand next to the door. "Pick that shit up." Stunna picked the bags up in preparation to follow Chico "What's that in plastic bag homie?"

"Snacks a diversion you never know who might be watching" Stunna nodded toward the door. Chico grabbed the bag grabbing a Arizona Iced Tea leading Stunna to some sliding doors that he opened.

"Sir this is him."

There were two men in the room one white and the other dude look Arabic they were both dressed to the tee. Stunna wondered how so many nationalities got together but shit if it worked for them it would damn sure work for him. He hopped the brother wasn't in the kitchen somewhere he chuckled to himself.

"Finally!" The Arabic began "I was beginning to think you don't want any money."

"You was thinking the wrong shit."

"Perfect."

"So"

"So?"

"I got my bag do you got yours?"

"Oh yes yes straight to the point I like that. Get him the bag." The white guy grabbed a bag from the side of the couch he sat at. Big Chico picked it up and carried it over sitting it at Stunna feet. Stunna grabbed for the bag.

"No no no same time we look in bag." Stunna handed his bag to Chico who carried it over to the white guy. "Now you may open or whatever, thirty kilos of cocaine.

"Money Money Money Moonnnaaayy!"

"I like him. Yes it is for today for tomorrow and many many years to come. How about a celebration drink?" The white man's phone began to ring and he stood up "Take it later it's a celebration." The white man excused himself "Always been a party pooper he doesn't get excited of money like me."

"Why even be in this business then."

"He's crazy"

"My dick get harder to money then pussy these days" Arab laughed real hard to Stunna's truthful words

"FREEZE"

"What the…"

"Don't you fucking move, you are under arrest."

"I didn't nothing I'm just here having a drink."

"With cocaine sitting snuggled right up under you huh and not the user amount either."

"I want my lawyer."

"You want a lawyer huh for what again, having drink?"

"Fuck you Cracka."

Stunna knew exactly what this was. All the wrong he did all the confusion he had done. Thinking Concrete would actually pick him over X. He couldn't help but just laugh.

Niecy Waved X down as she stood in front of Sam and Eddies with her pistachio gelato.

"Woman I just seen you bout two weeks ago and your stomach was not looking this big."

"Whatever still fine plus I just stuffed my face with pizza. It's a pizza baby." Niecy said rubbing her belly when she looked up she noticed Concrete pulling around with the car she reached in her bag pulling out the zip lock bag and opening it. "It's a poem I wrote you for your birthday." X grabbed the letter "Concrete and I are going to miss you. He is the lover I never could of dreamed of and your like my brother I never had. I hope whatever yall going through it can be fixed." Concrete was pulling up behind X "There's my knight in shining amour. See you around Xavier."

X watched as Niecy hoped in with Concrete. He made an illegal U-turn hit is horn and stuck his arm out with a peace sign and just like that they were gone. He almost felt like he wanted to cry but he didn't because he remember Niecy's poem. He opened it and read

X,

Blood I know you mad at me and all that's why I had Niecy contact you and deliver this letter. I know just like me you have a hard time telling her no right along with the love and respect you have for her. That's why we both love you like wed do.

Xavier do not hate me. What I did the other day was for the both of us and then some and this letter will explain it all. First Stunna's take down that was me. I always hated that nigga but dealt with him off the strength of you. The thought of him really thinking of killing you and me over a connect was him creating his own hit and all while forgetting that the streets talk. Second you know I love my wife and would do anything for her. So she the reason I got to go, her and that seed. Third my word is my bond you should know that. The Plug is yours in a matter of speaking you are the Plug big dawg.

Tomorrow as planned you'll be meeting with the man himself Jorge Luis he is a Peruvian and this man is cold blooded. We get a kilo of pure cocaine for eight hundred because of our business history and how we always adding more territory which brings more money. Yes brother the profit always been there that's why I try to let everybody eat.

Something to know about Jorge Luis, he is a very simple man. Pay him what is owed no matter what happened to product pay him. He will pluck off your family if he feel disrespected he does not care. He will only deal with you once you send someone in your place that money is gone. Due to all the years in the game all our operation is part of an internal conspiracy you got all type of law enforcement to TSA down to government

officials on pay roll. The whole Central and Southern Florida is yours. You are the infamous Creep. Every state county worker and associate is listed. Memorize everything then burn all this shit.

A big smile spread across Xavier's face

Made in the USA
Monee, IL
11 December 2020

52327064R00059